Dear Miiya, !

Your year 5 teachers.

SHERLOCK HOLMES

THE SIX NAPOLEONS

SIR ARTHUR CONAN DOYLE

Chapter One

'The summer is almost here,' said Lestrade, staring into the fire. 'Yet the weather is still so cold.'

I looked up at him and smiled. 'I hear it will get warmer towards the end of the month.'

Detective Lestrade of Scotland Yard often spent the evening with us. Sherlock Holmes liked his visits and was always interested in hearing about his latest cases. Sometimes he would even give Lestrade a hint to help solve them.

We had been sitting in silence for most of the evening. Lestrade was puffing on his cigar and Holmes was buried behind his newspaper.

At last, Holmes looked up. 'Do you have any interesting cases at the moment, Lestrade?'

'No, not really, Mr Holmes,' he replied.

'Go on, tell me,' said Holmes.

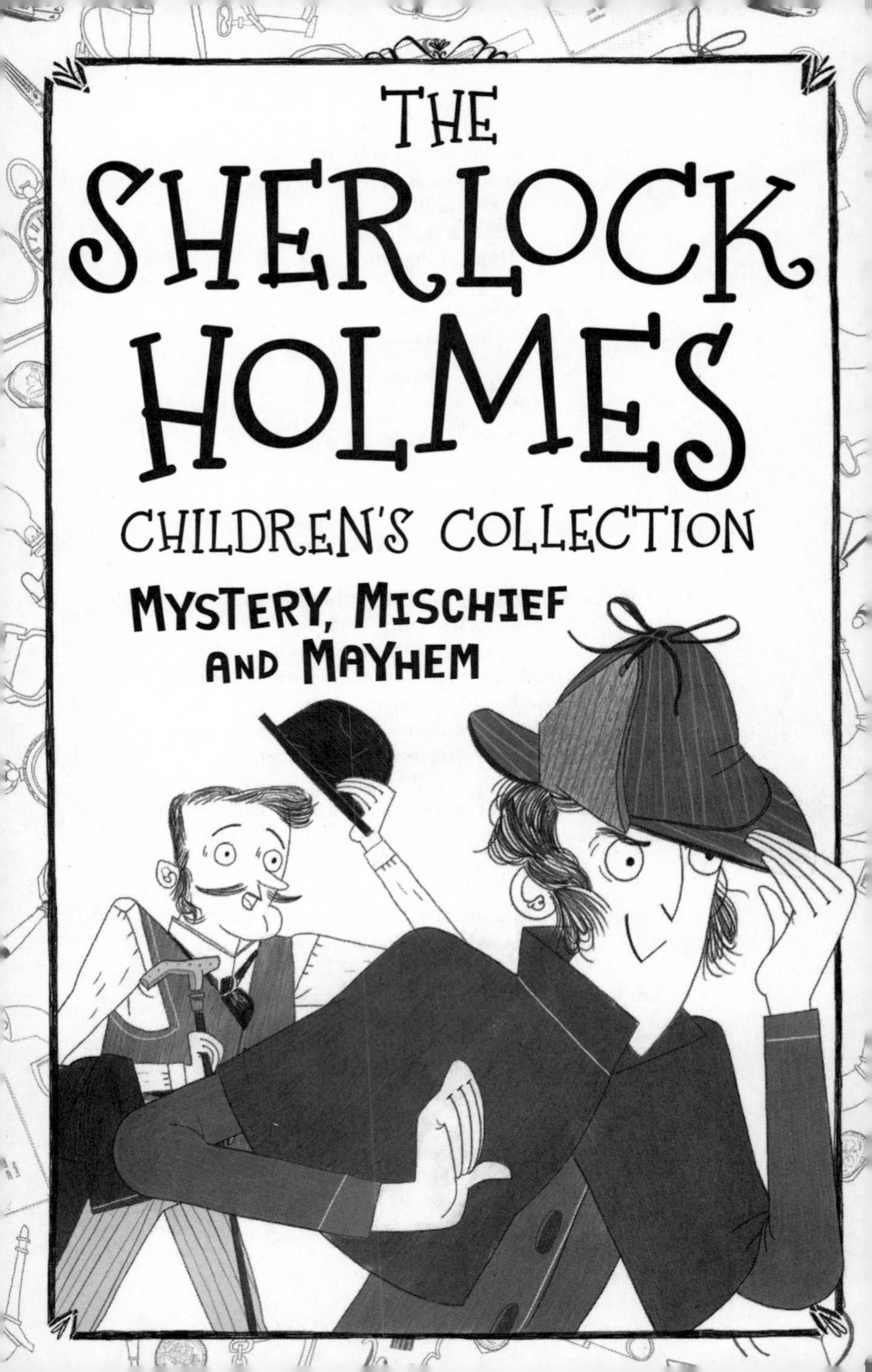
THE SHERLOCK HOLMES
CHILDREN'S COLLECTION
MYSTERY, MISCHIEF AND MAYHEM

Published by Sweet Cherry Publishing Limited
Unit 36, Vulcan House,
Vulcan Road,
Leicester, LE5 3EF
United Kingdom

First published in the UK in 2020
2021 edition

2 4 6 8 10 9 7 5 3

ISBN: 978-1-78226-422-4

Sherlock Holmes: The Six Napoleons

Based on the original story from Sir Arthur Conan Doyle,
adapted by Stephanie Baudet.

Cover design by Arianna Bellucci and Rhiannon Izard
Illustrations by Arianna Bellucci

Lexile® code numerical measure L = Lexile® 660L

Guided Reading Level = W

www.sweetcherrypublishing.com

Printed and bound in India
I.TP002

He could tell that Lestrade was holding something back.

Lestrade laughed. 'Well, Mr Holmes, I can't deny that there *is* one case on my mind. But it's so silly that I wouldn't want to bother you with it. It's more a case for Doctor Watson, if anything.'

'Something to do with disease?' I asked.

'Maybe not disease, but definitely madness. You wouldn't think that there was anyone who still hated Napoleon Bonaparte.

Well, hated him so much that they would break any pictures they found of him.'

Holmes sank back in his chair. 'That's nothing I can help with,' he said.

'Exactly. That's what I thought. It's really a matter for a doctor to deal with. But when that same person commits burglary, that makes it a matter for the police.'

Napoleon Bonaparte

Napoleon Bonaparte was a French military commander, who became Emperor of France. He tried to expand the size of France's armies and led many people to war. Because of this, many people dislike him. However, others think that he is one of history's greatest military leaders.

Holmes sat up again.

'Burglary! This is more interesting. Let me hear the details.'

Lestrade took out his notebook and flicked through the pages.

'The first case was four days ago,' he said, reading from his notes. 'It happened at Morse Hudson's shop.

He sells pictures and statues in Kennington Road. The assistant left the front of the shop for just a minute when, suddenly, he heard a loud crash. He hurried back in and found a statue of Napoleon, which had stood on the counter, smashed into pieces.'

Holmes was staring at Lestrade in deep concentration, the way he always did when he was listening to an interesting case. I put down my book and turned to face the detective. I did not want to miss a word of the story.

'The assistant rushed out of the shop to find the criminal, but he had disappeared. It just seemed to be one of those strange crimes that happens from time to time. It was reported to the police officer on duty. The statue was not worth more than a few shillings, though. So the crime didn't really seem important enough to investigate.

'The second case, however, was more serious and even more strange. It happened just last night.'

Chapter Two

Lestrade certainly knew how to tell a good story. Holmes and I were leaning forwards in our chairs, wanting to hear more.

'In Kennington Road, quite near to Morse Hudson's shop, lives a well-known doctor. His name is Doctor Barnicot. He has one of the largest practices in the south of England.'

Lestrade looked at me and I nodded. I had heard of this successful man.

'His home and main offices,' went on Lestrade, 'are in Kennington Road. He has another surgery and a pharmacy, too, in Lower Brixton Road. That's about two miles away. Doctor Barnicot is a big admirer of Napoleon. His house is full of books, pictures and old relics of the French Emperor. Not long ago, he bought two statues of Napoleon. Both were exactly the same and both were made by the

French sculptor, Devine. He put one statue in the hall of his house, in Kennington Road. He put the other statue in his surgery, in Lower Brixton.

'Well, when Doctor Barnicot came down this morning he found that his house had been burgled during the night. But, strangely, nothing had been taken – well nothing worth any money, that is. The only thing missing was his Napoleon statue. It had been carried out of the house and smashed against the garden wall.

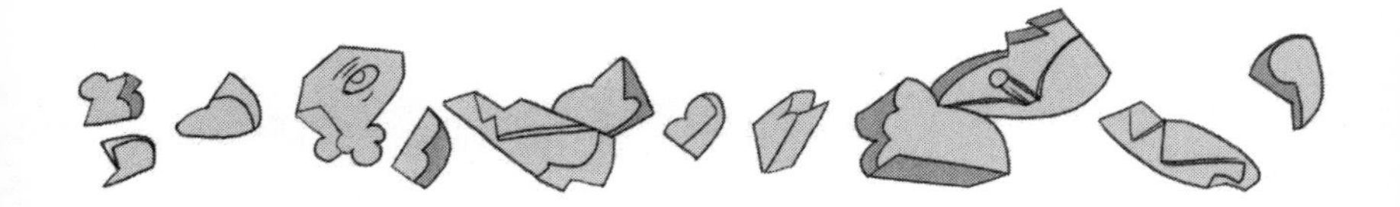

There was a pile of tiny pieces scattered across the ground.'

Holmes rubbed his hands together. 'This is certainly very strange,' he said.

'I thought you might say that,' Lestrade replied, smirking. 'But I have not got to the end yet. Doctor Barnicot was due at his surgery at twelve o'clock. When he arrived, he found that the window had been forced open. Broken pieces of the second Napoleon statue were scattered all over the room. There were no clues at the surgery or at the house to tell us who did it. Now, Mr Holmes, you have all the facts.'

'They are bizarre facts, indeed,' said Holmes. 'Were Doctor Barnicot's two statues exactly the same as the one in Morse Hudson's shop?'

'Yes, they were made from the same mould.'

'So the man who broke them does not just hate Napoleon. He wants to destroy those particular statues. There must be hundreds of statues of Napoleon in London. It would be too much of a coincidence that someone would destroy three of the exact same statue, just by chance.'

'Well, I thought the same,' said Lestrade. 'On the other hand, Morse Hudson, the owner of the shop, is the main seller of statues in that part of London. So, it could be that these were the only type of Napoleon statues in the area. What do you think, Doctor Watson?'

Something had come to my mind as he spoke. 'There is an illness that French doctors call an *idée fixe.* It's a sort of obsession.

Perhaps the man has read lots about Napoleon, or maybe his family was hurt by that war with the French. He might have formed an *idée fixe* obsession. It could make him want to destroy any image of Napoleon.'

I could see Holmes shaking his head.

'That won't do, Watson,' he said. 'No amount of *idée fixe* would allow the villain to know where to find the statues. Even if the obsession did make him want to destroy them.'

‘Well, how do *you* explain it?’ I snapped.

‘I don’t try to do so,’ he replied, smugly. ‘I would only point out that there is a certain cleverness in these mad crimes. For example, in Doctor Barnicot’s house, if the criminal had made a sound he would have woken up the family. So he took the statue outside before breaking it. While in the surgery, where there was less danger of someone seeing him, he smashed the statue where it stood.

‘This case seems so silly,’ continued Holmes, ‘But I cannot ignore it. Some of my most interesting cases began with simple, silly events.

‘So, I won’t laugh at the strangeness of your three broken statues, Lestrade. I would like to help, if I can. Please let me know if there are any new clues in the case.’

The clues Holmes asked for came quicker than we thought, and were much more tragic.

Chapter Three

I was getting dressed in my bedroom the next morning when there was a tap at the door. Holmes entered, with a telegram in his hand.

It read:

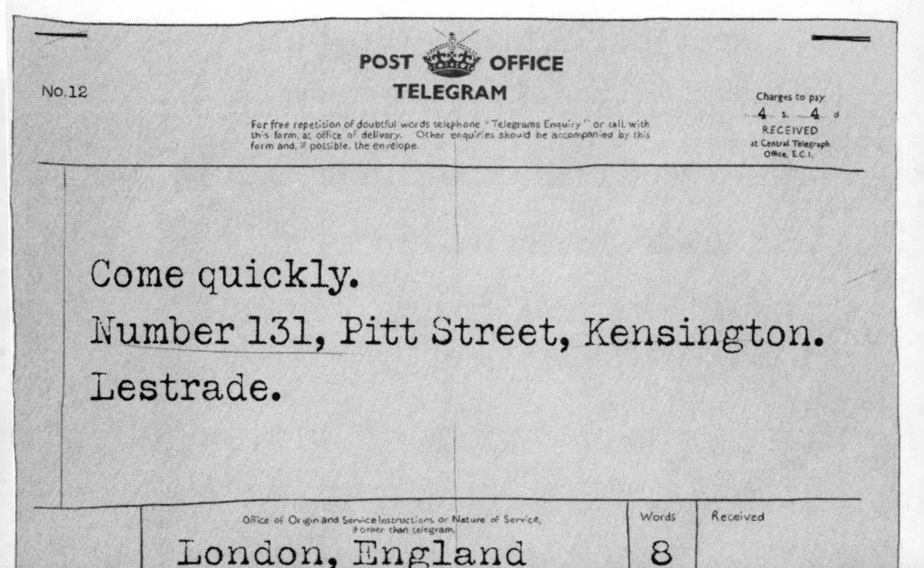

No.12

POST OFFICE
TELEGRAM

For free repetition of doubtful words telephone "Telegrams Enquiry" or call, with this form, at office of delivery. Other enquiries should be accompanied by this form and, if possible, the envelope.

Charges to pay 4 s. 4 d
RECEIVED at Central Telegraph Office, E.C.1.

Come quickly.
Number 131, Pitt Street, Kensington.
Lestrade.

Office of Origin and Service Instructions or Nature of Service, if other than telegram.
London, England

Words
8

Received

'What is it?' I asked.

'I don't know – it could be anything. But I suspect he has more to tell us about the story of the statues. There's coffee on the table, Watson. Drink it quickly because I have a cab at the door. Let's go.'

In half an hour we had reached Pitt Street. It was a quiet little street just outside one of the busiest parts of London. Number 131 was a small, ordinary house, that sat snugly within a long row of other small, ordinary houses.

They were all flat-fronted and tidy, but very plain. As we drove up, we saw that the house was surrounded by people. They were leaning their heads over the fence and peering through the railings, trying to work out what was going on.

Holmes whistled.

'By George! It must be attempted murder at least. Nothing less would stop a London message boy from working. He's even craning his neck in to get a good look. That tells me, Watson, that this must have been a very violent crime indeed.'

The cab stopped and we stepped out. We walked towards

London message boy

Children who are paid to deliver messages. Message boys are very common in London. They are very useful for getting messages sent across the city very quickly. If you pay them well, they will keep the message a complete secret, and even do a little spying on the way.

the house. The crowd parted for us, some looking curiously at Holmes and myself.

Holmes stopped and stared at the front steps. 'What's this, Watson? The top steps have been washed down, but the other ones are dry. Well, well, there's Lestrade at the front window. I'm sure he will tell us all about it.'

Lestrade met us with a very serious face and showed us into the sitting room. An angry-looking elderly man in his dressing gown was pacing up and down.

Lestrade introduced us. 'This is Mr Horace Harker,' he said. 'He's a journalist and the owner of this house. It's about the Napoleon statues again. You seemed to be interested in the case last night, Mr Holmes. So I thought you would be glad to help again, now that the case has taken a more serious turn.'

'What has it turned to then?' Holmes asked.

'To murder,' replied Lestrade. 'Mr Harker, will you tell these gentlemen exactly what happened?'

The man in the dressing gown turned to us with a horribly gloomy face.

'It's a strange thing,' he said. 'All my life I have been collecting other people's news. But, now that a real piece of news has come my way, I am so confused that I can't put two words together.'

He sighed deeply. 'If I had come here as a journalist, I would have interviewed myself. I would have had two columns in every evening paper. But now, I'm giving away a valuable story by telling it to every person who walks in the house. I suppose I can make no money from it myself.

'I've heard your name, though, Mr Sherlock Holmes. You could surely solve this mystery. To know the truth of it would be payment enough.'

Holmes nodded and sat down.

Mr Harker began his story.

'It all seems to be about that statue of Napoleon. I bought it for this room about four months ago. I picked it up cheap from the Harding brothers' shop.

'A great deal of my journalist work is done at night, and I often write until the early morning. I was doing so last night. I was sitting in my office, which is at the back of the top of the house.

At about three o'clock this morning I was sure that I heard a strange sound downstairs. I listened, but didn't hear it again. I thought that it must have come from outside. Then, about five minutes later, there came a horrible yell! It was the most dreadful sound that I have ever heard, Mr Holmes. It will ring in my ears as long as I live.

'I sat frozen still for a minute or two. Then I grabbed the fire poker and went downstairs. When I came to this room,

I found that the window was wide open and the Napoleon statue was gone. I could not understand why any burglar would want to take it. It was not worth any money.'

Holmes' eyes narrowed. He looked around the room, as if he were examining every tiny detail. I could tell that he was trying to put together the clues in his head. This case was getting stranger and stranger by the minute.

Mr Harker continued.

'I walked over to the window and peered out. I thought that I might be able to spot the burglar running from the house, but I couldn't. I couldn't see anything. So I went around and opened the front door, to see if he ran that way.

Stepping out into the dark, I nearly fell over a body lying there. I ran back for a light. I can barely speak about what I saw – it was too horrible. There was a poor fellow lying dead on the doorstep. I just had time to blow on my police whistle before I fainted. I must have fainted, because I remember nothing else. Not until I found a policeman standing over me.'

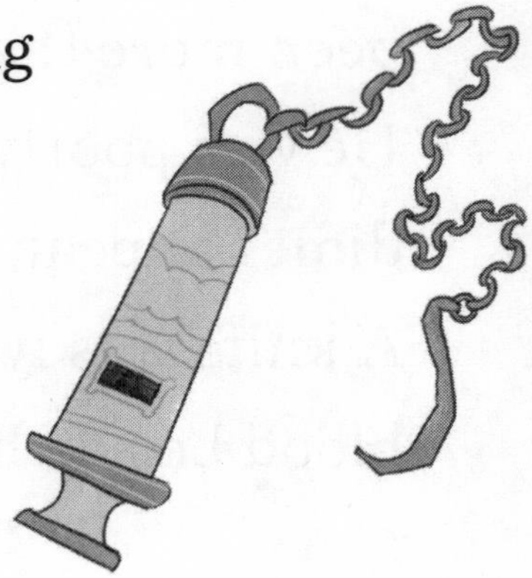

Chapter Four

'Well, who was the murdered man?' asked Holmes.

'We don't know,' said Lestrade. 'He was a tall, muscular man, with a suntan. He could not have been more than thirty years old. He was poorly dressed, but he didn't appear to be a workman. A knife was lying in a pool of blood beside him. I'm not sure if it was the weapon that killed the man or not.

'There was no name on his clothes. The only things in his pockets were: an apple, some string, a map of London, and a photograph. Here it is.'

Lestrade held out the photograph so that Holmes could see. I leaned over his shoulder to take a look, myself.

It had been taken by a small camera. It showed a sharp-faced man with thick eyebrows and a chin that stuck out quite far from his face.

'And what happened to the statue?' asked Holmes, after a careful study of the picture.

'We found it just before you came. It was in the front garden of an empty house in Camden House Road. It was smashed into tiny pieces. I am going to see it now. Will you come?'

‘Certainly,’ said Holmes, rising from the chair. ‘But first, I must just take one look around the house.’

He examined the carpet and the window. ‘The criminal must have very long legs or be very active,’ he said. ‘It would not have been easy to reach that high window ledge and open the window. Getting out would have been much simpler. Are you coming with us to see the remains of your Napoleon statue, Mr Harker?’ Mr Harker had seated himself at a writing table. He shook his head.

'I must try to write something about this mystery,' he said. 'Although I know that the evening papers will already have printed the full details. It's just my luck! I'll be the last to report on a murder done on my own doorstep.'

As we left the room, we heard his pen scratching wildly against his paper.

The place where the broken statue had been found was only a minute's walk away. The splintered shards of the statue lay scattered across the grass.

Holmes picked up several pieces and examined them carefully. I was sure from the look on his face that he had finally found a clue.

'Well?' asked Lestrade.

Holmes shrugged. 'We have a long way to go yet,' he said. 'And yet … and yet … well, we have some facts to think about. To the criminal, getting hold of this statue was clearly worth more than a human life.

Then there is the odd fact that he did not break it in the house, or just outside the house. He waited until he had walked down the street.'

'He must have been distracted by meeting this other fellow,' said Lestrade. 'He hardly knew what he was doing.'

'That's probably correct,' replied Holmes. 'But look at the position of this house, where the statue was smashed.'

Lestrade looked about him.

'It is an empty house, so he knew no one would see him.'

Holmes nodded.

'Yes, but there is another empty house farther up the street,' Holmes said. 'He must have passed that one before he came to this one. Why did he not break the statue there? Every step farther he carried it, he was risking someone seeing him.'

'I give up,' said Lestrade. 'Why did he break it here then?'

Holmes glanced at me, smiling, and I pointed to the streetlamp above our heads.

Holmes nodded. 'He could see

what he was doing here, but not there. That was his reason.'

'By Jove! That's true,' said the detective. 'Now that I come to think of it, Doctor Barnicot's statue was broken not far from his lamp. Well, Mr Holmes, what are we to do with this fact?'

'To remember it – to make a mental note. We may find out something later on that connects to it. What steps do you think we should take now, Lestrade?'

'We must find out who the dead man is on Mr Harker's doorstep.

That shouldn't be difficult. When we have found out who he is and who his friends are, we should be able to work out why he was in Pitt Street last night. And, most importantly, who killed him. Don't you think so?'

'Most definitely. But it is not quite the way I would work,' replied Holmes.

'What would you do, then?' asked Lestrade.

'Oh no, do not just do things my way! You should do it your way and I will do it mine. We can share notes afterwards.'

'Very good,' said Lestrade.

Holmes turned around as we were about to leave. 'If you are going back to Pitt Street,' he said, 'please tell Mr Horace Harker that I have made up my mind. It's certain that a dangerous murdering madman, with a Napoleon obsession, was in his house last night. It will be useful for his article.'

Lestrade stared. 'You don't seriously believe that?'

Holmes smiled.

'Don't I?' he replied. 'Well, perhaps I don't. But I am sure that it will interest Mr Horace Harker and the newspaper readers. Now Watson, I think we have a long and difficult day's work ahead of us.'

He turned back. 'I should be glad, Lestrade, if you could meet us at Baker Street at six o'clock this evening. I need your help with something. If I'm correct, it is something that *must* be done tonight. Until then I would like to keep this photograph that was found in the dead man's pocket. Goodbye and good luck!'

Chapter Five

I had worked out one or two things about the case. But Holmes, as usual, was far ahead. We walked together to the high street. Holmes stopped at the shop of the Harding brothers, where Mr Harker had bought the Napoleon statue. A young assistant told us that the owner, Mr Harding, would be away until the afternoon. He said he, himself, had only just started working at the shop, so could not give us any information. Holmes' face twisted in annoyance.

'Well, well, we can't expect to have it all our own way, Watson,' he said at last. 'We will come back this afternoon, when Mr Harding is at the shop. It is important that we work out where these statues came from. I am sure it will lead us to discover the strange reason why they are all being smashed. I think we should visit Mr Morse Hudson, the owner of the shop in

Kennington Road. He might be able to offer some answers.'

An hour's drive brought us to the picture dealer's shop. Mr Morse Hudson was a small, round man, with a red face and a grumpy attitude.

'So, the Napoleon statue was taken from your shop?' asked Holmes.

'Yes, sir. From my very counter, sir. What we pay taxes for I don't know, when there are no police about to stop criminals coming in and breaking my things. Yes, sir, I sold Doctor Barnicot his two statues, too. The whole matter is horrible, sir! What kind of man would go about breaking statues for no reason?'

'Who did you get the statues from?' Holmes asked, ignoring the man's angry rant.

'What has that got to do with it?' snapped Mr Hudson. 'If you really want to know, I got them from Gelder and Co. in Church Street, Stepney. They are a well-known company. They have been about for twenty years.'

'And you bought just three statues?'

He nodded. 'Three, yes. Two and one are three. I sold two to Doctor Barnicot and one was smashed here. In broad daylight! On my counter!'

Holmes took out the photograph he'd kept from the dead man's pocket. He placed

it on the counter in front of Mr Hudson.

'Do you know this man?' Holmes asked.

'No, I don't,' he said, looking quickly at the photograph. Then he looked again. 'Actually, yes, I do. It's Beppo. He's an Italian man. He used to work for me in the shop. He could carve a bit, and gild and frame, and do other odd jobs. He left me last week. I've heard nothing from him since. I don't know where he came from or where he went to, but he was a good worker. He left two days before the statue was smashed.'

Holmes thanked him and we left.

'Well, that's all we could really expect to get from Morse Hudson,' said Holmes as we came out of the shop. 'This Beppo man appears in both crime scenes, in Kennington and in Kensington. That information was surely worth the drive.

'Now, Watson, let's take a trip to Gelder and Co. of Stepney.

That's where the statues were made. I think we will find some answers there.'

We quickly passed through the fashionable side of London. Past the big hotels, the theatres, and the shopping sector. Finally, we arrived at London docks. Here, huge blocks of houses were huddled together. Then, a little further along, in a broad street, we found Gelder and Co.

It was unmissable. Outside the building lay huge piles of stone and marble. Inside, we found a large room where fifty workers were carving and moulding, with hammers and chisels. The sound was horrible!

The manager, a large bald German man, greeted us in a friendly manner. He showed us into his office so that we could talk without the noise.

He was happy to answer Holmes' questions. He told us that they had made hundreds of Napoleon statues. Each was an exact copy of

a famous sculpture of the head of Napoleon. The three that had been sent to Mr Morse Hudson had been half of a batch of six. The other three in that batch were sent to the Harding brothers of Kensington.

'I can't think why anyone would want to destroy them,' the man said with a laugh. 'We sold them for just six shillings. And I can imagine the shop keepers would have only sold them for twelve.'

‘How are they made?’ asked Holmes.

‘We take a plaster cast from each side of the original marble statue. Then we join these two pieces together to make the statue. The work is usually done by artists, in that room.’ He pointed to the big room we’d just left. ‘When the statues are finished, they are put on a table to dry. Then once they’re dry, they’re stored away.’

Holmes showed the manager the photograph he'd found in the dead man's pocket. The man's faced turned red with anger. His brows knotted over his blue eyes.

'Ah, the rascal!' he cried. 'Yes, I know him very well. This is a good company. The only time we have ever had the police here was because of this man. It was more than a year ago now. He stabbed another man in the street. Then he came straight to work, would you believe it? But the police were chasing him. He was arrested right here. Beppo was his name – I never knew his second name. Serves me right for hiring a man with no references. But he was a good workman: one of the best.'

'What prison sentence did he get?'

'He was allowed to live, and got off with a year in prison.

He must be out by now. But he has not dared to show his face here. A cousin of his works here. He could probably tell you where Beppo is.'

'No, no!' cried Holmes. 'Do not say a word to the cousin. I beg you. It is very important that he does not know we're on to him.

'Could you just give me the date when Beppo was arrested?'

'I could tell you roughly by the paylist,' the manager answered. He reached for a book and flicked through the pages. 'He was last paid on the twentieth of May.'

'Thank you,' said Holmes. 'I don't think I need to take up any more of your time. Please keep this conversation private.'

We left again, walking through the noisy workshop and out into the fresh air.

Chapter Six

It was quite late in the afternoon before we were able to get a quick lunch at a restaurant. There was a newsstand at the entrance. The newspaper headline read:

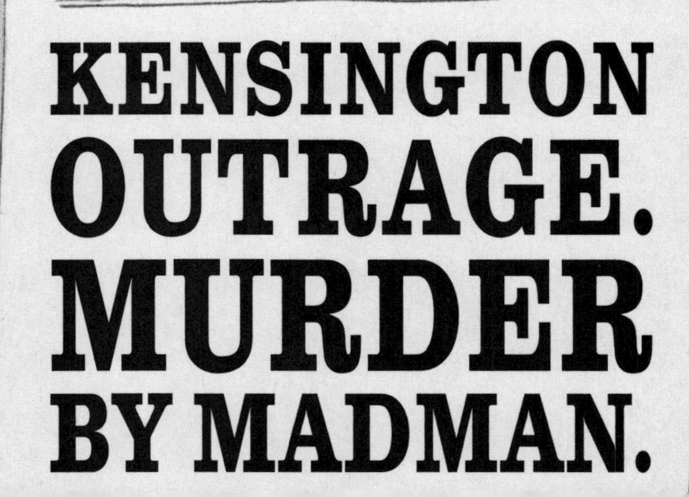

KENSINGTON OUTRAGE. MURDER BY MADMAN.

The contents of the paper showed that Mr Horace Harker had got his article into print after all. There were two columns of his very dramatic report. I smiled as I thought about how Holmes called *my* writing dramatic, but I didn't comment on it.

Holmes had bought a newspaper. He propped it against the salt and pepper stand and read it while he ate. Once or twice he chuckled.

'Look at this, Watson,' he said.

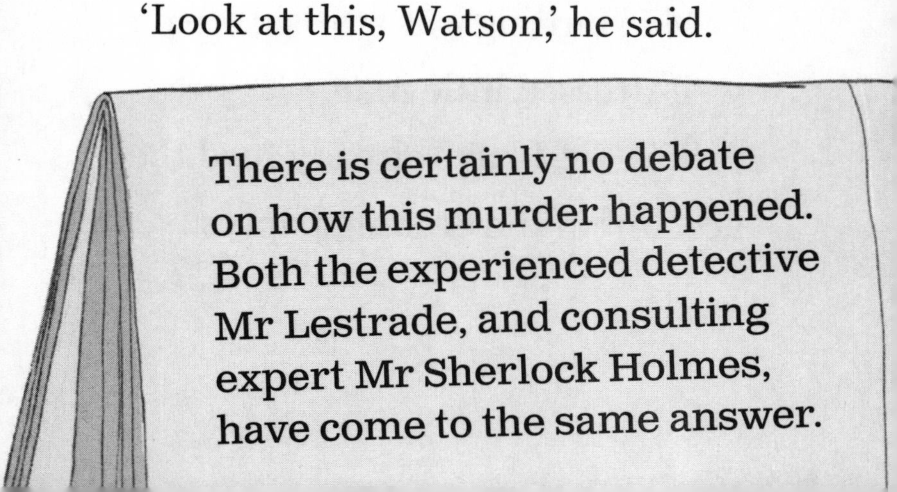

There is certainly no debate on how this murder happened. Both the experienced detective Mr Lestrade, and consulting expert Mr Sherlock Holmes, have come to the same answer.

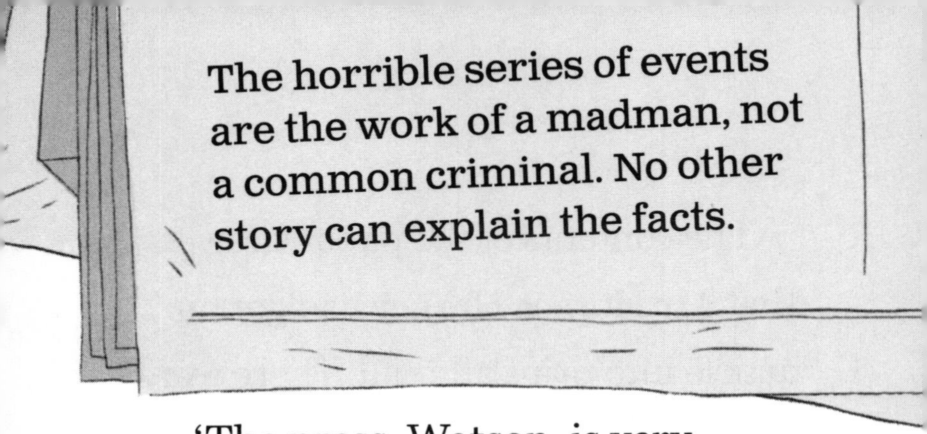

The horrible series of events are the work of a madman, not a common criminal. No other story can explain the facts.

'The press, Watson, is very valuable, if you only know how to use it. And now, if you have finished your lunch, we shall go. Let's head back to Kensington. Mr Harding should be at his shop now. Let's see what he has to say on the case.'

Mr Harding was a brisk, crisp, well-dressed little man.

'Yes, sir, I have already read the account in the evening papers.

Mr Horace Harker is a customer of ours. We sold him the Napoleon statue some months ago. We ordered three statues from Gelder and Co., of Stepney. They are all sold now.'

'To whom?' asked Holmes.

Mr Harding looked a little annoyed. 'Oh, if I just take a look at our sales book, I can easily tell you,' he said. He pulled a large book off a shelf behind him.

'Yes, here we are. We sold one to Mr Harker, and one to Mr Josiah Brown of Laburnum Lodge, Laburnum Villa, Chiswick. Oh, and the last one went to Mr Sandeford of Lower Grove Road, Reading.'

Holmes pulled out the photograph, again. Mr Harding shook his head.

'I have never seen that face,' he said. 'I would remember if I had.'

'Do you have any Italians on your staff?' asked Holmes.

'Yes, several of our workmen and cleaners are Italian.'

'And you keep the sales book there, so anyone can look at it?'

'There's no reason to keep a careful watch on it,' Mr Harding replied, confused.

As he walked us out of the shop, Mr Harding said, 'It's a very strange business, this is. I hope you will let me know if you find any answers.'

Holmes had taken notes while Mr Harding was talking. I could see that he had deduced something from the facts we had learned. He did not tell me what he had discovered, though. He only said that, unless we hurried, we would be late for our meeting with Lestrade.

Sure enough, when we reached Baker Street, Lestrade was there. We found him pacing up and down, impatiently. The smug look on his face showed that he must have discovered another clue.

'Well,' he asked. 'Have you had any luck, Mr Holmes?'

'We have had a very busy day,' said

my friend, 'and not an entirely wasted one.' Holmes invited us all to sit down.

'We have met the shop keepers and the people who made the statues. I now know the whole story of the smashed statues.'

'The statues!' cried Lestrade. 'Well, well, you have your own methods, Mr Holmes. I won't say anything against them. But I think I have done a better day's work than you. I have found out who the dead man is.'

'You don't say so.'

'And found a cause for the crime,' Lestrade added, smugly.

'Splendid!'

'We have an inspector, Mr Hill, who works just in the Italian Quarter. Well, the dead man had a Catholic symbol around his neck. That made me think he was from the south.

'Inspector Hill knew him the moment he saw him. His name is Pietro Vanucci. He's from Naples, and he is one of the greatest cut-throats in London. He is connected to the Mafia which, as you know, is a large group of criminals. They often use murder to scare people into doing what they say. Now, you see, the mystery is starting to clear up.

'The murderer is probably an Italian also, and another member of the Mafia. He must have broken the Mafia's rules in some way. Pietro was probably sent to track him down. The photograph we found in his pocket would be

Cut-throat

A killer, who murders people by cutting their throats. A cut-throat will often be part of a group of gangsters, criminals, or even the Mafia.

to remind him who he was looking for. Pietro follows the fellow, sees him enter a house, and waits outside for him. But, in the scuffle, Pietro himself is killed. How about that, Mr Sherlock Holmes?'

Holmes clapped his hands. I could see that he was pleased with this progress.

‘Excellent, Lestrade, excellent!’ he cried. ‘But you did not explain why the statues have been destroyed.’

‘The statues! Get those statues out of your head. That crime is nothing: petty theft, six months in prison at the most. It is the murder that we are really investigating. I tell you that I am close to having all the evidence.’

‘And the next stage?’ asked Holmes.

‘Is a very simple one. I shall go with Inspector Hill to the Italian Quarter. We will find the man from the photograph. Then we will arrest him on a charge of murder. Will you come with us?'

'I don't think so. I am sure we can solve this case in a simpler way. I can't say for sure, though. It all depends on one small thing that is out of our control. But I have great hopes – in fact, I'm almost sure we will succeed. If you will come with us tonight, Lestrade, I will help you catch the criminal.'

'In the Italian Quarter?'

'No. In Chiswick. If you will come with me to Chiswick tonight,

I promise to go to the Italian Quarter with you tomorrow. How about that, Lestrade?'

Holmes looked at me and then back at Lestrade, again. He clapped his hands together. 'Now, I think that a few hours of sleep would do us all good. I plan to leave at eleven o'clock this evening and it's unlikely that we will be back before morning. You can dine with us, Lestrade. Then you are welcome to nap on the sofa until it is time for us to leave.

'In the meantime, Watson, please ring for an express messenger. I have a letter to send, and it is important that it should go at once.'

Holmes scribbled a short letter. I didn't peek over his shoulder, even though I was desperate to see what he had written. Instead, I rang for Mrs Hudson and asked her to call a messenger boy.

Holmes spent the rest of the evening flicking through the old newspapers in our attic. When at last he came back down, he looked very pleased with himself.

But he didn't tell either of us what he had found.

I had followed Holmes' methods, step by step. Though I had not yet worked out the answer to the case, I'm sure Holmes had. I understood clearly that he expected the criminal to try to destroy the last two statues. One of them, I remembered, was in Chiswick. It was obvious we were going to Chiswick to try to catch him in the act. Holmes had cleverly given Mr Harker the wrong clue for his newspaper story. This meant the criminal thought he was safe, and could continue his evil plan without anyone finding out. I was not surprised when Holmes told me to bring my gun. He had picked up a loaded hunting crop, which was his favourite weapon. It seemed that Holmes thought this criminal was very dangerous.

Loaded hunting crop

This is my favourite weapon. It's a sort of whip. It is a long, straight stick with a hook at one end and a small leather loop at the other. A loaded hunting crop is filled with metal to make it heavier and more dangerous.

Chapter Seven

A four-wheeler coach was at the door at eleven o'clock. It drove us to a spot on the other side of Hammersmith Bridge. Here, the cabman was asked to wait.

We took a short walk to a quiet road that was lined with pleasant houses. Each house stood in the centre of a huge garden.

In the light of a streetlamp we

read *Laburnum Villa* on the garden gate of one of the houses. The people who lived there all seemed to be in bed. The house was completely dark, apart from a small window over the front door. It shone a single blurred circle of light onto the garden path. A wooden fence separated the house from the road and threw a thick black shadow over the garden. We crouched and hid in the darkness of that shadow.

'I think that we might have a long wait,' said Holmes. I heard Lestrade sigh. He did not like waiting.

‘We may thank our stars that it’s not raining,’ went on Holmes. ‘I don’t think we should even smoke to pass the time, as it will give away our position. But all the waiting will be worth it, believe me.’

Our wait was not as long as Holmes had thought. It all happened very quickly.

In an instant, and without a whisper of sound, the garden gate swung open. A slim, dark figure rushed up the garden path.

We saw him fly past the tiny spot of light from the window and disappear against the black shadow of the house. There was a long pause. We held our breath. Then a very gentle creaking sound came to our ears.

The window was being opened. The noise stopped. There was another long silence. The man was breaking into the house. We saw the sudden flash of a lantern inside the room. Then we saw the flash of light through another blind, and then another. It seemed he couldn't find what he was looking for.

'Let's get to the open window. We can grab him as he climbs out,' Lestrade whispered.

But before we could move a muscle, the man came out of the house again. As he walked out into the small, glimmering patch of light we saw that he was carrying something under his arm. Something large and white. He looked around him. The silence of the empty street made him think he was alone. Turning his back on us, he laid down what he was carrying. The next second we heard a sharp tap, then a clatter and a rattle.

The man was so concentrated on what he was doing that he never heard our steps as we crept across the grass.

With the pounce of a tiger, Holmes was on his back. Lestrade and I grabbed him by his wrists and fastened handcuffs around them.

We turned him over. A sallow face with angry features, glared up at us. I knew that this was indeed the man in the photograph.

But Holmes was not looking at our prisoner. Kneeling on the doorstep, he was looking at what the man had brought from the house. It was a statue of Napoleon like the one that we had seen that morning. It had been broken into pieces, just like the others. Carefully, Holmes held each piece up to the light. It looked to me just like pieces of shattered plaster.

Holmes had just finished inspecting the pieces when the hall lights turned on. The door opened, and the owner of the house stepped forwards. He was a jolly-looking man, with a round body. He was already fully dressed.

'Mr Josiah Brown, I suppose?' said Holmes.

'Yes, sir, and you must be Mr Sherlock Holmes? I got the note that you sent by express messenger, and I did exactly what you told me. We locked every door on the inside and waited silently. Well, I'm very glad to see that you have got the rascal. I hope, gentlemen, that you will come in and have a drink.'

Lestrade, however, was keen to get his man to the police station. So, within a few minutes, our cab came to pick us up and we were on our way back to London.

Our prisoner said nothing. He simply glared at us from under his hair.

His clothes were searched at the police station. They found nothing more than a few shillings and a long knife. The handle of the knife was stained with blood.

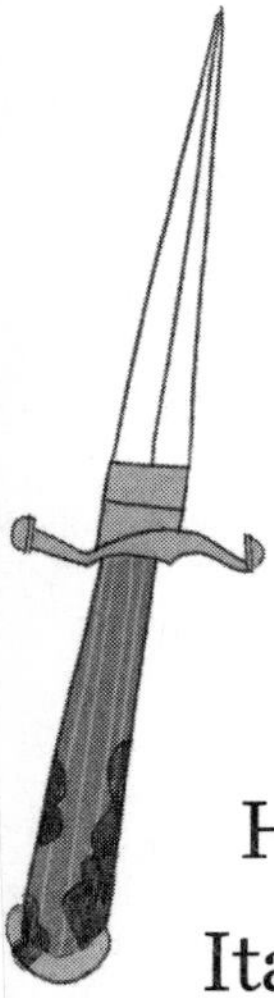

'That's all right,' said Lestrade as we left the station. 'Inspector Hill knows everyone from the Italian Quarter. He will be able to tell us who this man is. I bet you'll find that my theory about him being in the Mafia is right. But I'm very grateful to you, anyway, Mr Holmes. Your plan let us catch him much quicker than we might have. I don't quite understand it all yet, though.'

'Ah, I fear it is too late for explanations,' said Holmes.

'Besides, there are one or two details that are not yet clear.

'If you can come to my rooms at six o'clock tomorrow, Lestrade, then I can explain everything. It truly is one of the most curious cases I have come across.'

He looked at me with a twinkle in his eye. 'I may, one day, Watson, allow you to write a report of the cases I find trickiest. I think if you did, the strange adventures of the Napoleon statues would make a great read.'

Chapter Eight

When we met Lestrade the next day, he gave us more information about the prisoner.

His name, it seems, was Beppo. His second name was unknown. He was a well-known rogue within the Italian community. He had once been a great sculptor and had earned an honest living. But he turned to evil ways. He had been to prison twice already. Once was for petty theft and the other, as we knew, was for stabbing a fellow countryman.

He could speak English very well, but he wouldn't talk about the statues. We still had no idea why he wanted to destroy them. The police thought that he may have made the statues himself, since he was a sculptor at Gelder & Co.

Holmes listened to all this information, though we knew some of it already. I could see that Holmes' mind was elsewhere. He seemed uneasy. He looked as if he were waiting for something to happen.

At last there was a ring at the door. Holmes gave a slight jump in his chair. His eyes brightened. A minute later we heard steps on the stairs and an elderly, red-faced man was shown in by Mrs Hudson. In his right hand was a large, old-fashioned bag. He placed it on the table.

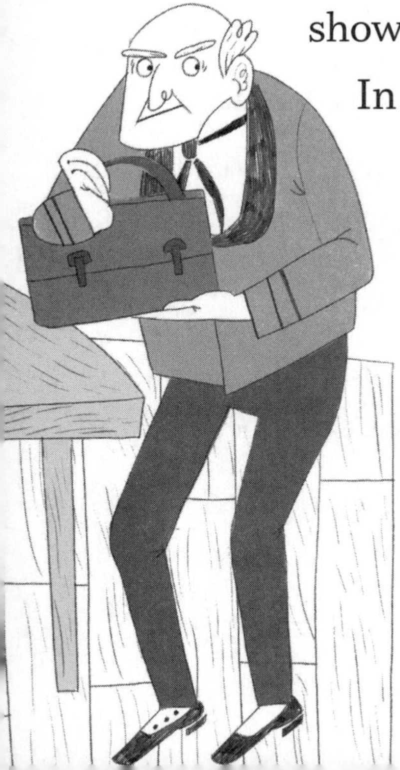

'Is Mr Sherlock Holmes here?' he asked.

My friend bowed and smiled. 'Mr Sandeford of Reading, I suppose?' he said.

'Yes, sir. I fear that I am a little late, but the trains were delayed. You wrote to me about a statue that is in my possession.'

'I did.'

'I have your letter here.' He pulled the crumpled letter from his pocket and showed it to us.

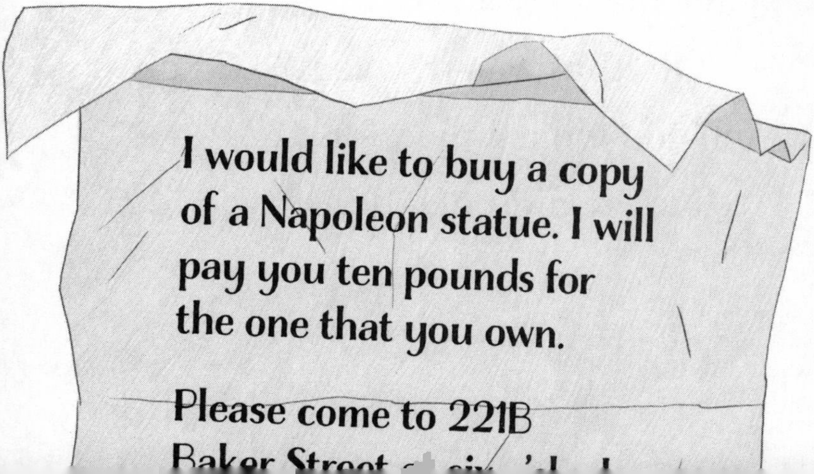

I would like to buy a copy of a Napoleon statue. I will pay you ten pounds for the one that you own.

Please come to 221B Baker Street

'Is that right?' the man asked.

'Certainly,' Holmes replied.

'I was very surprised at your letter. I have no idea how you knew that I own a Napoleon statue.'

Holmes nodded. 'Of course, you must have been surprised. The explanation, though, is very simple. Mr Harding said that he had sold you their last one. He gave me your address.'

'Oh, that was it, was it? Did he tell you what I paid for it?'

'No, he did not.'

'Well, I am an honest man, though I'm not a very rich one. I only paid fifteen shillings for the statue. I think you should know that before I take ten pounds from you.'

'I named that price, Mr Sandeford, so I intend to stick to it.'

'Well, it's very good of you, Mr Holmes. I brought the statue with me, as you asked me to do. Here it is!'

He opened the bag and at last we saw, placed upon our table, a complete Napoleon statue. It was a very good sculpture, I thought.

Holmes took a paper from his pocket and put a ten pound note on the table beside it.

'Can you just sign that paper, please, Mr Sandeford. It is just to say that you have sold the statue to me, and do not have any right to it now.'

Mr Sandeford signed the paper. Then Holmes thanked him, paid him the money and said goodbye.

When our visitor had gone, I opened my mouth to speak but thought better of it. Holmes suddenly started acting very strangely. Strangely even for Holmes.

He began by taking a clean, white cloth from a drawer and laying it on the table. Then he placed the statue on the cloth. Finally, he picked up his loaded hunting crop and struck the statue on the top of its head.

We gasped as the statue shattered into tiny pieces, just like the others. Holmes bent over the smashed statue.

'Ah ha!' he shouted, holding up one small piece to the light. It had a round, dark object in the middle.

'Gentlemen!' he cried. 'Let me introduce you to the famous black pearl of the Borgias!'

Chapter Nine

Lestrade and I sat in silence for a moment. Then, suddenly, we broke out clapping.

Colour sprang to Holmes' pale cheeks. He bowed to us like a magician who had performed a clever magic trick.

It was at such moments that he stopped being a logical thinking machine. Just for a minute, he showed his human side – he loved being admired.

'Yes, gentlemen,' he said, 'it is the most famous pearl in the world. It has been my good luck that I have been able to find it.

'Using deduction and logic, I followed the pearl's journey. From the Prince of Colonna's bedroom at the Dacre Hotel, where it was lost, to the inside of this statue of Napoleon.'

Lestrade and I looked closer at

the blue-black gem that Holmes held between thumb and first finger. It was perfectly round and about one centimetre wide.

'You will remember, Lestrade,' Holmes went on, 'the drama this jewel caused. London's police failed to find it. I was even consulted on the case, but couldn't figure out the answer. Everyone thought that it was stolen by the maid of the princess, who was an Italian. She has a brother in London.'

Lestrade nodded. 'Lucretia Venutti,' he said.

'Indeed,' said Holmes. 'There is no question in my mind that this Pietro, who was murdered two nights ago, was the maid's brother. I looked up the dates in the old newspapers. The pearl vanished exactly two days before Beppo was arrested at Gelder & Co. for stabbing the countryman. It happened at the very moment when these statues were being made.'

I was beginning to see where the story was going.

'Beppo had the pearl in his possession,' Holmes continued. 'He may have stolen it from Pietro or maybe he was his partner in crime. He may have been the one who passed a message between Pietro and his sister. It doesn't matter to us which is correct.

'The main fact is that *he* had the pearl at that moment when he was being chased by the police. He ran to the factory where he worked. He knew he only had a few minutes to hide the valuable gem. He couldn't have it on him when he was searched, or they would send him to prison for that, too.

'Six statues of Napoleon were drying in the passageway and one

of them was still soft. Beppo made a small hole in the wet plaster, dropped in the pearl, and then smoothed it over. It was a clever hiding place. No one could ever find it.

'But Beppo was sent to prison for a year. While he was there, the six statues were sold all over London. He did not know which one contained the pearl. So he could only find it by breaking each statue.

'Beppo was clever about it. His cousin, who works for Gelder & Co., told him which shops had bought the statues. Then he took a job with Morse Hudson, so that he could see the sales book and track down who three of the statues were sold to. He found and broke all of those, but the pearl was not there. Then, with the help of an Italian employee, he found out where the other three statues had gone. The first was at Harker's. He went to Harker's but met his partner in crime there, Pietro. Pietro thought it was Beppo's fault they had lost the pearl. So they fought, and Beppo stabbed Pietro.'

'If Beppo was Pietro's accomplice, then why did he need to carry his photograph? Wouldn't he know what he looks like?' I asked.

'It's so he could show the photo to other people and ask them if they'd seen him,' Holmes replied.

'Well, after the murder, I was sure that Beppo would speed up his search. He would fear that the police would guess his secret. Of course, I did not know if he had already found the pearl. He may have found it in Harker's statue. I was not even sure that it was the pearl. But I was sure that he was looking for something. He carried the statue past a whole row of houses, just to find an empty one with a light next to it. It's clear that he wanted to inspect the statue carefully when he broke it.

'Then there were only two statues left. It was obvious that he would go for the London one first. I warned the people who owned it, so that they were on guard when Beppo broke in. Then, as you know, we were able to catch him. By that time, of course, I knew that it was the Borgia pearl that we were after. The name of the murdered man linked the one event with the other. There was only one statue left – the one in Reading – so the pearl must be there. I bought it from the owner, and here it is.'

We sat in silence for a moment.

'Well,' said Lestrade, 'I've seen you work on many cases, Mr Holmes, but this one beats the lot. We're not jealous of you at Scotland Yard. No, sir, we are very proud of you. If you would come down tomorrow, there's not a man in the force who wouldn't be happy to shake your hand.'

'Thank you,' said Holmes. 'Thank you!'

He turned away, but I did not miss the smile on his

face, or the glistening in his eyes. I had never seen him display such human emotions before. I felt very fond of him at that moment.

When he turned back, he was the cold and practical man once more. 'Put the pearl in the safe, Watson,' he said. 'Then get out the papers of the Conk-Singleton forgery case.

'Goodbye, Lestrade. If any little problem comes your way, let me know. I shall be happy to help solve it.'

Lestrade shook hands with us both and left.

Sherlock took his violin out of its case. He began to play a strange, dreamy tune. I lit my pipe and settled down to read the paper.

Sherlock Holmes

World-renowned private detective Sherlock Holmes has solved hundreds of mysteries, and is the author of such fascinating monographs as *Early English Charters* and *The Influence of a Trade Upon the Form of a Hand.* He keeps bees in his free time.

Dr John Watson

Wounded in action at Maiwand, Dr John Watson left the army and moved into 221B Baker Street. There he was surprised to learn that his new friend, Sherlock Holmes, faced daily peril solving crimes, and began documenting his investigations. Dr Watson also runs a doctor's practice.